A Close

Prince of Darkness

Jerry Francis

Special Thanks

Jane, my wife of over 62 years, has stayed by my side in all seasons of our marriage. She has helped me with this venture by reading many times over the various drafts and correcting many mistakes. Thanks, honey.

Accolades and gratitude go to my son Ron, who is a published author. I can only say that there would be no book without him. The scores and scores of times he "fixed" my computer and tried to teach me how to save something to a flash drive would put most people over the edge. His help, suggestions, and patience spanned the entire project. Thanks, son.

Many thanks to Dr. Marc D. Baldwin of Edit911.com for his invaluable assistance with the editing process.

Special thanks to Dorian of sitesvalley.com for the excellent cover design.

Table of Contents

Preface

This booklet was written for men and women of all ages, religions, and persuasions. It is an attempt to meet all of us right where we are now. It is designed to cause us to reflect on what is going on deep within our hearts. That is "**the home**" that the author is speaking about in this account of a self-willed person who lived on life's razor's edge. The Lord was never far from the main character in this allegorical account, but the reverse was not so. He was not aware that he was infected with a disease that would one day destroy him.

A casual reading might result in missing the point altogether. This is a love story between God and the people whom He created, and it reveals how He is always pursuing us. It is His desire either to keep His people from falling into a dark pit or to take them out of the deep hole that they dug for themselves. Even when God the Father seems to be coming off "hard" because of disobedience by His people (children), this is the side of His love that human parents call "tough love."

A Close Encounter with the Prince of Darkness addresses the needs of everyone because, in one way or another, all of us have failed to live as we should. Everyone needs His loving attention, correction, and perhaps even a total or significant change deep within their being. That includes some who call themselves Christians. While this story is dedicated to a young person, we all know how stubborn and set in their ways older folk can be.

Many people of our day do not see the Christ in His people. They see hypocrisy or a religion that is not culturally modern or relevant. Jesus was and always will be counter-cultural, so, in that respect, their views and lives do need that significant change. On the other side of the coin, Christians in their lifestyles should be displaying the Love of God in a powerful way to give those on the outside a fair chance to make the right choice regarding the real Christ. There is a saying that is true: the people of faith might be the only bible that others have ever read. So, if we who are called by His name are not at a spiritual place or not in right standing with our Savior, our words, deeds, and "opinions" drop to the ground rather than dropping into a needy heart.

John Carter, the main character in the story, wasn't a bad person per se. Without a doubt, he had the qualities of a being a helper as well as being a hero type, but that gift or quality was overshadowed by too much "self-garbage." John was not a believer, but he was loved.

Often, the story will include references to the Bible written in italics. Some of the verses were copied from the Bible to prove that the accounts presented throughout the fictional narrative are confirmed by the facts and truths that come from the Highest Authority. Some of the verses were copied from the New King James Version of the Bible and others were paraphrased to emphasize an important biblical point.

A Close Encounter with the Prince of Darkness is not meant just to give biblical facts or to be a Bible study aid. It is a book intended to come alongside us in a positive way. Everyone will be able to take their "spiritual temperature" to see whether they are in good shape for the journey ahead and to know for sure that they will arrive safely on shore at the

Father's Home. Also, situated within the pages of this allegory is a poem titled, **"He Danced with Me,"** which the author believes deepens the message of the story.

Included in the back portion of this booklet is a perfect description of the love that God has for us and His offer to all mankind captured in a writing titled, **"Behold our God."** Then, at the end of the book, there is a powerful litany that sums up **"The Passion of the Christ"** in a way that will stir the heart of any open-minded reader. All three of these passages give supporting evidence to the biblical truths expressed in the encounter. They were included to present those truths in a picturesque and poetic form and style.

The Bible is a people book from beginning to end. It is a written record of the character and nature of God. It was designed to show and teach us many things. Its truths are not meant to bring harm, but it includes strong warnings for all who do not think that they need a change in their lives or believe that they can take their gift of "free will" that God gave them and do whatever they want without being bound by God's attempts to intervene in their lives.

He desires to come alongside us on our journey. His Word was given to lead, guide, protect, heal, and bring us victory throughout our lives. He desires for all people to learn to communicate with Him. The Bible is up-front and personal, friends. Don't read this booklet from a position of fear. It is the opposite of a hellfire and damnation message.

There is an encouraging scripture that gives an idea of how much love God had for both the main character in the allegory and has for us. It is found in the Old Testament, *Isaiah 46:4*, which says, "I will be your God throughout your lifetime. I made you and I will care for you."

This brings to light another truth that will be expressed in this short story and is recorded in the Old Testament, in *Jeremiah 29:11*, which says, in essence, that His thoughts and plans for us are to promote our welfare or peace rather than bringing us harm or causing us disaster and to bring us a future filled with hope. Who doesn't want to have a future that brings with it verifiable hope? Well, for many years John Carter lived as one who did not have that hope. John Carter was going to need a significant change. John Carter was going to have to die. All who seek assurance that they are on the path to **God's home** are encouraged to look beyond this encounter and go to the Bible for confirmation and direction.

A Close Encounter with the Prince of Darkness is an easy read and you do not need to have a doctorate in theology to grasp its intent and purpose. All the best, Jerry.

Chapter One: The Beginning

As a young man, John Carter always wanted to do things his way. Over the years, his pattern of expressing self-will would cause him to make many poor life choices. John could be described as an intelligent, friendly, but stubborn type of guy. However, because he was truly a rebel filled with his own ideas, he was actually "dumb-smart," a person who seems intelligent but does foolish things. Though everything he did seemed right to him, at the end of the day, John often was pursuing a literal dead-end trail (*Proverbs 14:12, 14*)

Every wild adventure that he engaged in was against his parents' advice or orders—when he even bothered to inform them what he was doing. He always accepted his punishment like a champ, but, afterward, he would continue his foolhardy schemes. If John Carter got something in his head, he ran with it. Often, his mother would cry out within herself, *Oh, Johnny, why? Why, son?*

Walter and Betty Carter had three boys. They never had any problems with Kevin, their firstborn, or their youngest, Roger. It was always John. Because John believed that he was a "free spirit" type, he felt that he had the right to make his life choices without listening to the opinions of others. He had four close encounters with death. Finally, he met Death's Author head-on and found that he was ill-equipped to fight for his very soul.

Chapter Two: Tommy

It was a cold wintry day after a light snowfall had covered the entire region. Crisp air dominated the early evening hours. John and his buddy Tommy Blackburn had decided to go to a club on the other side of the mountain from where they lived. When they arrived and got out of their car, gusts of wind blew in their faces and through their light jackets. As they neared the entrance to the building and heard the laughter and noise coming from inside the Rooster Rod and Reel Club, their excitement mounted. Once inside, they presented their 'fake ID's' which were easy to get, and seldom scrutinized closely.

The boys knew that the trip would be worth their time and money. Both enjoyed the friendly atmosphere. John spent most of the night at the dartboards. He destroyed his opponents every time he played. He had a great eye for the game and a deadly aim that was not hindered by the beer that he was consuming. He also enjoyed spending time at the bar talking, especially to the senoritas. Tommy loved to do his drinking and dancing with a beer in one hand and his arm around the waist of a pretty girl. At 3 am, John leaned over the barstool and told his buddy that he was feeling beat. "So am I," Tommy replied, "let's vacate the joint." The night had passed quickly, and they had a long ride home.

Tommy had a lead foot and had already received several citations for speeding from local law enforcement. On this night, he got the bright idea to shorten the two-hour trip home and make it an hour and a half. True to form, when they got into his car, he accelerated to the max, spraying a trail of icy dust and gravel across the front of the parking lot. He made a right turn onto a back road and again put the pedal to the metal. He was now racing along a dark stretch covered with ice and frozen slush. With one hand on the wheel and the other wrapped around a beer, he sped the vehicle over the mountain roadway.

The car kept twisting and turning as the tires slid over the patches of frozen blacktop. Tommy and John shouted and laughed as their favorite music blared. Tommy bragged to his buddy in a slurred voice, "Did you see the one I was dancing with? The one wearing the short green dress. She had green eyes too, I think. Wow! I gotta see her again."

Up ahead was a sharp 40-degree left-hand curve, one of many twists and turns on that back road. Though he had driven the route many times, Tommy's boozed-drenched brain forgot about the turn, which was preceded by a slight dip and then a rise. He was doing nearly 100 mph when his car came to the frozen bend.

Proverbs 23:30-32 are among the many Old Testament verses that warn us about what can happen when people linger at the wine table. In the New Testament, *Ephesians 5:18* warns us that excess drinking will ruin our lives, and *John 2:6-10* describes how Jesus turned the water into wine—unsurprisingly, He did not do so for chariot drivers to crash on the way home from that wedding feast. The people who drank that evening were still responsible for their conduct, just like Tommy and John.

Tommy failed to negotiate the turn. With no traction, the car went airborne. It seemed as if it had been launched from a

16

huge catapult and was spinning sideways. The occupants were not laughing anymore. The next sound that John heard was a terrific crash and the crunching of metal. Then came blackness. A huge oak had brought the car to a sudden stop.

Tommy was killed instantly, and John was knocked unconscious. It took a while for the emergency services to arrive because of the isolated location of the wreck and the treacherous road conditions. When the paramedics, police officers, and firemen arrived, they had to use the "jaws of life" to extricate John from what was left of the car, the rest of which was pressed flat against the tree. By the time he was free of the car, he was awake but dazed. Everyone at the scene wondered how he had survived, for the car was wrapped like a horseshoe around the old oak about six feet off the ground. The ambulance took him to the hospital for x-rays and to remove fragments of glass from his face, arms, and legs.

Hours later, John called his father to ask for a ride home. It was about 11 am when his parents arrived at the hospital. When they heard about Tommy's death and smelled the booze on their son, they could think of nothing to say. It was a long and quiet ride back home. Once again, Betty Carter asked herself as she wept silently, *Why Lord? What's going on with John? I know you have a plan for his life, but surely this is not it!* Walter Carter, on the other hand, felt an icy anger toward his son rising within him.

At the funeral, John couldn't bring himself to look at Tommy's body in the coffin. He could barely manage to look at his family. He was sad about his friend's death and wept openly. However, there was no change on the inside. John was still John. Except for driving a little fast, he saw nothing wrong with the way he and his friend had been partying. *After all,* he reasoned, *everybody likes to unwind and have a relaxing evening.* He could not or would not look at the big picture that was right in front of him. Instead, he talked about his "good fortune" and "lucking out."

This pattern of ignoring his parents' advice at every turn was repeated in his dealings with other figures of authority in his life. The problem went beyond his lack of common sense. Something was wrong or missing inside this young man. Being wild at heart seemed to energize what was going on deep inside him.

The morning after the funeral, John's father took the keys to his car and gave him a bike to get around on. His anger remained, but he wanted to try and start over with his son. During the driving suspension, John and his father went on a hunting trip as they had many times in the past. Walter Carter desperately hoped that some father-son time would help him to identify or connect with his boy or at least understand him better.

Chapter Three: Leslie

A new family moved into town, and the daughter, Leslie, began attending John's school. He offered to give her a ride when she needed one. He even went so far as to introduce himself to her parents and ask their permission. He also told his parents about it. Leslie was 16 years old and very smart but also very naïve.

After John had become quite friendly with Leslie and their relationship had grown past simply being school pals, he asked her to come with him to Jessie's Joint, a local entertainment center that had food, drinks, games, and a dancefloor and, of course, John's favorite indoor sport, darts. The bar was usually jammed with people. The huge sign over the entrance to Jessie's Joint read, "Y'all come and have food and fun." Leslie had become enamored of this handsome young man with smooth talk and a winning smile, which, along with a couple of kisses, convinced her to go with him after class. They didn't ask their parents' permission. John knew that some rough characters made Jessie's their second home. He talked up the food to convince Leslie to go with him but really wanted to show her how good he was at darts.

They had a quick bite to eat, and John then took Leslie by the hand and led her to the dartboards. Leslie was very impressed at his skill as she watched from about ten feet away. Behind her were a large, seedy-looking fellow and his drunken friend sitting on a nearby stool. The large man had a disheveled appearance, with unkempt hair and beard. Motioning to his buddy, he made an outline of Leslie's body with his gyrating arms and hands while smacking his lips together. When his friend laughed and said, "Go for it, Homer!" he came up behind Leslie and grabbed her in a bear hug. With his arms tight around her waist, he bent over and, leaning his head against hers, started kissing her neck. She could smell the stench of booze and his bad breath. In a low voice meant to be sexy, he whispered into her ear, "Come on honey, let's dance!" as she protested and tried futilely to break his grip. Terrified, she burst into tears and began calling out "Help me, John, please."

John was about to toss a dart when he heard her cry and turned to see the seedy-looking character pawing his girlfriend. He dropped the dart and ran over to punch the bearded groper in the face. The buddy jumped up from the bar stool and tried to hit him with a chair but struck Leslie's arm instead. She screamed in pain. A side kick to his stomach from John took him down. The big drunk let Leslie fall and rushed at John, knocking him over a table and then kicking him in the face as he tried to rise. The kick only enraged John, however, and he leaped up and side-kicked his attacker's leg. John followed through with a short snapping forearm blow to the throat, and Homer went down like a sack of potatoes.

The owner of the establishment emerged from his office and pushed past the curious onlookers. Seeing what had happened and that John and Leslie were just kids, he shouted "What the — is going on here?" Realizing that he didn't want any more trouble, in an angry but nervous tone, he told them "Get outta here and don't come back!" No one called an ambulance or the police. John drove Leslie to the hospital. It turned out that her arm was broken, as was his nose. As soon as he could, he called her parents, the police, and his father.

Both sets of parents arrived at the hospital at the same time. When the police told them what had happened, Leslie's parents were in shock and demanded of Walter and Betty, "What kind of people are you?" They wanted to know why they had so little control over their boy that he would even think of taking their daughter to such a disreputable place and were convinced that John had tricked her, taking advantage of her youth. In front of John's parents, they asked Leslie whether she had ever been "touched" by him. Leslie said no but admitted to a few kisses. Angry accusations were hurled at John to the effect that he was a wolf in sheep's clothing. While *Matthew 7:15* did not apply to their son, John and his parents still got the point.

John's mother was openly crying, and his father was so angry that he struggled not to hit his son. Walter tried to apologize to Leslie's parents but a short, "I don't want to hear it," from her father put an end to his effort. Leslie wept and asked her parents' forgiveness for not calling them and for acting so stupid.

The two thugs plead guilty in criminal court and received a suspended sentence. A huge fine was levied against Jessie's Joint in civil court. Jessie paid it and all the medical costs. His place was closed for three months by court order. Neither set of parents participated in the civil action.

Leslie was just a teenager and lacked street smarts and, in her heart, knew that she should not have gone anywhere without first asking her parents. She had been fully aware, though, that they would not approve of Jessie's Joint. John knew very well that he should never have taken her anywhere without all the parents agreeing. The bottom line was that he, too, knew that they would not have approved the afternoon visit to Jessie's.

Nevertheless, John was not remorseful. He believed that he had not done anything particularly bad. In fact, he had defended Leslie when she needed it. He was sad when he learned that her parents had enrolled her in a private school and forbidden her to see him and said that they would take out an order of protection if he went against their wishes.

And, if he disregarded the protection order, they would formerly charge him with stalking their daughter and the police would arrest him.

Proverbs 14:12 is a key verse that recurs throughout this booklet because of its importance for all of us and not just the main character in this story. The verse reads, "There is a way that seems right to a man, but its end is the way of death." In this case, the death involved a budding friendship. At the "end of the day," what John really needed was steadfast attention, discipline, and structure and not just a lecture or a punishment that did not fit the crime.

John was angry when his father told him that he needed to see a counselor. He refused, and the subject was not brought up again. At this point, Walter and Betty should have insisted that he seek help. John later regretted not following through with the idea of getting help from someone outside his family, and so did his parents.

Exodus 20:12 is a commandment to people of all ages to "Honor your mother and father that it may go well with you" (paraphrased). The many infractions and stupid things that

John did that did not turn out well were evidence of the truth that he was not honoring his parents.

Chapter Four: Discipline = Love

The Bible has a lot to say about what can happen when children do not follow God's ways or the advice of those He has ordained to care for and counsel them. If we do not instruct our children and show them the right way, then, the Word of God says, we do not truly love them. *Proverbs 13:24* puts it this way: "He who does not punish/discipline/correct/ his son when he needs it does not love him but hates him" (paraphrased), and this, of course, applies to girls as well. The reason for such strong language is because, ultimately, parents who do not properly discipline and train their children will end up raising sons or daughters who will become rebellious and lead a "fractured life" that, in one way or another, will cause harm to others and themselves. How can we say that we care about them when we know early on that they keep wanting their way about something that we as parents have already said no to? When we surrender our rights as parental leaders, our children will take the reins and, ultimately, get their way. We as parents must ask ourselves, if they are not following our orders or advice who are they listening to? Who or what is influencing them?

Love and discipline go together as the proper way to train a child—the focus cannot be simply on punishing them. However, sending children to their rooms so that they can text their friends or play on the computer [called giving them a 'time out'] is not the right way to train or punish them for breaking the rules or doing something wrong. It is the path toward ruining them.

Parents must obey the Lord's ways, and children must obey their parents (*Colossians 3:20*). This does not sit well with us because we do not like people "ordering us around." Why is it that parents in Africa or Norway or Brooklyn or anywhere else on the planet must teach their sons or daughters, "no-no, don't touch" when they want to do or take something that they shouldn't? They don't have to teach them "yes-yes" because that comes naturally to us. Many times, we want what we want when we want it. Just watch the news on TV, and you will see the truth of this.

In John's case, his mother and father were always trying to get him to see the light, and they did try to give him the special attention that he needed. However, they never could quite figure out what was missing or what they had done wrong. The truth was that they did not consistently follow through with the correct type of discipline. Punishment alone or yelling was not the answer, and they saw that this approach was not changing their middle son. It was time for them to be creative, but they often missed opportunities to do so.

They did know that he was AWOL from the Lord and headstrong, but the root cause of the problem escaped them because often he was so kind and offered help to those in need. He also was a smooth talker and could deceive or "con" his parents easily. He was used to his mother crying and his dad yelling. He had their number because they were so predictable.

Despite their son's behavior patterns, though, the family was not dysfunctional. They were warm and kind to each other. Their friends from church often stopped over for dinner, and laughter could be heard as they enjoyed each other's company. Most people who knew John liked him. They just thought he was a little wild. He also liked them but did not think that they were cool. As for church itself, he could take it or leave it. Eventually, he got what he wanted and left.

Chapter Five: A Mixed Bag

John, like all of us, was a "mixed bag." Not everything he did was born of a know-it-all attitude, nor were all his ideas bad. Sometimes, he showed creativity, talent, and determination.

On a hot afternoon in late June, the Carters' phone rang. R. J. Farnum, a farmer from the nearby town of Tavares, was calling to ask whether John wanted to do some major repair work on his old barn. Young John was delighted at the opportunity and started the next day. After surveying the situation, he could see that it was going to be a design issue including the loft supports as well. It was a major project. John asked, "Mr. Farnum, do you mind if I completely change out those two huge front and back doors and reframe the openings and work on the loft?" The farmer replied, "Go to it, boy." John worked there for over two months. He rented machines and hoists and special tools. He drew pictures of what he thought the barn should look like when the job was complete. On a couple of occasions, Mr. Farnum assisted him. When the job was complete, the farmer inspected it. It was far beyond what he had expected. In fact, he was amazed. John received a generous paycheck and a strong handshake that said, "Thank you."

Shortly after John finished the barn job, Walter and Betty got a visit from Mr. Farnum. He knew about some of their son's escapades and troubles. "Walt, Betty," he said, "John did an incredible job. When it came to those broken-down sets of doors and the sagging loft, your boy tackled the problem head-on. He showed such innovation and skill when putting his repair plan into action. It was like he saw the job already complete in his mind's eye." He paused and then said, "I don't know, but perhaps he just needs to be kept busy. Anyway, I'm gonna keep him on my prayer list." With that, he shook Walter's hand, nodded at Betty, and took his leave. Afterward, they went into prayer to thank the Lord for their friend's encouraging visit and commitment to pray for their son. They also told John about the visit and what Mr.

Farnum had said, but he just shrugged his shoulders and asked, "What's for dinner, mom?"

One of the things that gave them hope was that their son did sincerely like to help others. In a nostalgic moment, Betty recalled with her husband the time when John had risked his life trying to save a little boy who was trapped in a burning car. He was driving on Highway 27 in his dad's truck on the outskirts of nearby Leesburg when he saw the vehicle in front of him swerve off the road and plunge down an embankment. He quickly stopped and ran down the hill. The car had rolled over and settled at the bottom of a ravine in flames. He found the car upside down and heard a young boy crying. Leaning in through the shattered window, he took out his six-inch knife and cut the seatbelt. Just as he was pulling the boy from the wreck, the rear seat where he had been riding burst into flame. Walter and Betty became weepy as they recounted the near-tragedy and how John had made light of it. They learned most of the story from the local newspaper account. Apparently, the young boy's father had had a fatal heart attack behind the wheel.

John wanted to work through that entire summer, so he put an ad in the local paper. He had no problem getting jobs because many people, including folks from his church, knew him to be a good worker. A neighbor about twenty miles to the south called him about another barn job that would entail a little repair work, cleaning out the loft, raking loose dirty hay in and around the area into a pile, and bagging all the debris. It seemed like an easy assignment and promised to pay well. He did not know the farmer, but he took the job.

When he arrived, he met Mr. and Mrs. Jones and their six-year-old daughter Ruthie. The farmer explained what he wanted. A few hours into the job, John had raked everything into a large pile in front of the barn. The sweat was running down his face, so he wiped his eyes and decided to take a rest under a shady tree nearby. As he was about to do so, he heard a squeaky little voice call out to him and looked up to see a frightening sight. Little Ruthie had placed a towel around her neck to form a cape. "Look at me!" she said to John. "I can fly. Wee, here I go!"

In a panic, John raced toward the twenty-foot-high loft where the girl was standing just as she raised her hands high and dove headfirst off the ledge. At the same time, he too dove into the pile of dirty hay just under where he figured that she would land, turning his body face-up in the hopes of breaking the girl's fall and grabbing her.

Claudia Jones heard a scream from inside the house. Her husband Harold was working about seventy-five yards away and heard it also. Both raced toward the barn. When they got there, little Ruthie was sitting on John's chest crying. John was in severe pain and whimpering. Blood was coming from under his collarbone and shoulder. Two of the four curved prongs from a rake that had been partly buried in the pile of hay had pierced his upper body.

Claudia ran back to the house to call for an ambulance. Harold picked up the child and tried to steady the pole that the rake was attached to. It was hard to do because John was writhing in pain. In a loud voice, the farmer said to him, "John, John, you're going to have to try and hold steady or you may do more damage to your chest, son." It was not just his chest, for his neck was also wounded.

A tortuous forty minutes passed between the call to the hospital and the arrival of the ambulance. The pain was numbing John's mind, and he kept whimpering softly and seemed to be laboring to breathe. Claudia told the paramedics that he had lost a lot of dark-colored blood. The hospital staff notified the doctor on call, and they arranged to administer plasma on the return ride back. First, they had to stabilize him.

Harold's arm was tiring as he and one of the paramedics held the rake tight while another carefully cut through the two-inch-thick handle of the rake with a saw from a nearby shed. John received an IV and strong pain killers. An x-ray of his chest and neck in the hospital would assess the damage where the young girl had landed after her flight.

Harold Jones called Walter and Betty and told them what happened. John's entire family arrived an hour and a half later along with Pastor Joe Toro from their church. Mr. and Mrs. Jones arrived with little Ruthie as John was undergoing emergency surgery.

Two hours later, Dr. Johnson, the operating surgeon, came into the waiting room and reported that John was in stable condition and expected to recover. His collarbone was broken, and a small bone chip from his shoulder had lodged in a muscle in his upper arm. His neck, though, was relatively unscathed thanks mainly to Mr. Jones' holding the rake steady. The doctor explained that, with all the nerves, arteries, and veins in that area, John could have easily died. The x-ray showed no serious damage to his chest from the impact of Ruthie, but the whole area was badly bruised. John was unable to receive visitors until the following day since he was in a deep sleep. The normal visiting hours were 2 pm to 8 pm, and the family planned to be there early. Pastor Toro said a prayer of thanks to the Lord and then invited the Joneses to church on Sunday. They accepted the invitation. Everyone left for home, but the drama wasn't over.

At 1 pm the next day, as his family members were preparing to go see John, a call came from the hospital. A surgery nurse reported that John had developed a very high fever. but the cause was unclear. Because his body was clammy and his skin coloring didn't look right, he couldn't have visitors. He was being tested for tetanus because the rake had been rusty.

John's fever remained high, and, during the following night, he had a dream—or perhaps he was partially awake; he

37

wasn't sure. On his left, he saw ugly, dark, smelly, beast-like beings glaring at him and crouching like tigers ready to spring. On his right, he saw beautiful angelic figures in white with sashes around their waists looking at him with their hands raised high. The scene ended quickly, and the dream ended as he fell back to sleep. When he woke early the next morning, the fever was gone, and he was hungry.

The doctors examined him and, after running some more tests, said that he could be released in the afternoon. To their scientific minds, what had happened remained a mystery. John was excited. He called home to give his family the good news. He never told them about his dream.

What happened to their son was no mystery to his parents. It was the answer to their prayer directly from the heavenly Father's throne room. As *Jeremiah 33:3* states, "Call on Me, and I will answer you, and show you great and mighty things, which you know not." That was one of the verses that John's parents clung to during the ordeal.

John spent most of the summer months in a rehab center where, with the help of the therapists, he slowly recovered and built himself up. His encounter made the county papers, and he was interviewed by reporters several times, but he was more interested in getting well and didn't care about a story.

Every time he thought about the incident, he thought to himself, *I must be the luckiest guy on the planet.* He didn't perceive the connection between his survival and his parents' answered prayer, nor did he give any credence to the strange dream that he had had.

Later, during his encounter with Death, he would see its significance.

Chapter Six: Strike Three, John's Out

John Carter really did not like sitting through a church service, so he would go to the Sunday school class. This way, he could be with his friends and, if the opportunity arose, he could play the class clown. One Sunday, an elderly teacher, Brother Walt Christian, was teaching about the existence of God. In the middle of his discourse, John stood up and, pointing at him, demanded to know in simple language how he could prove that there was a God. John was performing for his peers by trying to put down his instructor.

Brother Walt was fully aware that John was trying to show off to please the crowd. In a calm voice, he asked the students to hold out their hands. He then pointed to the tips of his fingers and told them to do likewise. He told them that every person has unique fingerprints, which the police were able to use as evidence in criminal cases. The whole class, including the young wise guy, who was still standing, nodded. Before explaining to the class the significance of this fact, he said to John in an authoritative voice, "Why don't you sit down and join the class, son? You might learn something." Softly but confidently, he informed the students that there was no mathematical chance that such a situation could arise. No computer could calculate the odds of everybody having distinct prints. The explanation was that, when God created mankind, he created every person different from every other person on the earth. Just as DNA, which cannot be seen with the naked eye, proves the individuality of humans, so do fingerprints, which can be seen. God hand-crafted everyone, including everyone in the classroom, to be one-of-a-kind. All of this was done in the secrecy of the mother's womb. Further, he told the students, their unique fingerprints prove how valuable each person is individually and serve as evidence that they will not be passing through again. Everybody is equally important to the Creator. Brother Walt explained that there are many scriptures that point to God's existence. *Genesis 1-3* provides information about the existence of God and His creative abilities as well as the fall of mankind's first parents, Adam and Eve.

Brother Christian suggested that the class read these chapters. He then told the group that creation is just one of the ways to prove the existence of God. God himself went on the offensive regarding the matter, as is clear in *Isaiah 45:5*, "I am the Lord and there is no other. There is no God besides me," and *Psalm 14:1*, "The fool in his heart says there is no God." **Strike one!**

The whole class was just looking at John, who was now very quiet. After the class, some of the kids were pointing at him and laughing. This did not sit well with him. He did not like to be on the defensive, as is the case also later in his story. He resolved to prepare for his next encounter with his Sunday school teacher. Brother Christian had chosen as his topic whether the Bible was truly the word of God.

The following Sunday, John was ready for the 'debate.' To his surprise, however, Mr. Christian was not the teacher for the day since he was recovering from emergency knee surgery. Rev. William Vella, a noted biblical scholar, was filling in. John did not know him and thought that this would be a great opportunity to redeem himself by picking on the "new guy."

Rev. Vella had prayed for wisdom and that the hearts of everyone in the class be opened, but John ignored the prayer and went on the offensive. *I'm going to bury this old dude*, he told himself. Once more, he stood up and, in a loud voice, declared, "There were many bibles, so which one could people expect to believe? They say different things." To young John, variations in the text proved that the Bible was false.

In a calm voice, Reverend Vella thanked John for asking "a valid question" and went on to explain that few people know Hebrew and Greek, so the interpreters had to translate the ancient words into something that was readable. They also had to consider the world's various languages and cultures. The words have distinct meanings to people in various places. Additionally, the meanings of words change over time. Also, some Bibles are designed to be used for study. The teacher provided additional reasons for the variation but ended his explanation by pointing out that every Bible has the same intent and goal: to teach people the ways of God so they can make peace with Him and grow in Christlikeness and live a life that eventually leads them to the Father's home. In many places and ways, God has told us that he will instruct and watch over us. Thus, as *Psalm 32:8* says, "I will teach you and guide you in the way you should go" (paraphrased). The most direct way that He does this is through the Word of God, the Bible. John did not wait for the class to end but again left the room defeated. **Strike two!**

John Carter's last visit to Sunday school occurred the following week. This time, Brother Vic Irizarry was conducting the class. He was a retired law enforcement officer who had had a dramatic conversion to Christ many years ago and became an ardent student of the Bible. The topic for discussion was whether Jesus is God and the chosen Savior of the world. John again sat quietly waiting for his opportunity.

Brother Vic began by saying that there were scores and scores of prophecies in the Bible proving both that Jesus is Lord and that the Bible itself is true. He explained that, in Biblical times, if a prophet claimed that he was speaking for God and foretold things that did not come to pass, he would be taken out of the city and stoned to death. (Of course, this did not include his speaking about things that God said would happen centuries later.) God was not going to have any man speak falsely concerning Himself because He is a Holy God of truth and cannot tell a lie. Thus, for instance, *Numbers 23:19* and *Titus 1:2* are among other verses affirming that God cannot lie. He is, of course, far removed from our fallen human nature.

Mr. Irizarry listed only a few of the prophecies in hopes this would whet the appetite of the students for more verses, which they could quickly search for online.

PROPHECIES ABOUT JESUS THE CHRIST THE MESSIAH

He will be born in Bethlehem: Old Testament: Micah 5:2; fulfilled in the Matthew 2:1, 2.

The Messiah will be called Immanuel (God with us): Old Testament, Isaiah 7:14; fulfilled in Matthew 1:23.

The Messiah will be born of a virgin: Old Testament, Isaiah 7:14; fulfilled in Luke 1:31-35.

The Messiah's hands and feet will be pierced, and they will gamble for his cloak: Old Testament, Psalms 22:16-18; fulfilled in John 20:25-27.

The Messiah will be resurrected from the dead: Old Testament, Psalms 16:10, 49:15; fulfilled in Matthew 28:2-7, Acts 2:22-32.

The Messiah will be a sacrifice for sin: Old Testament, Isaiah 53:5-12, was fulfilled in The New Testament book of *Hebrews 9:26, Hebrews 10: 1-18.* [Numerous NT verse references.]

Again, it is impossible that one being could perfectly fulfill all these prophecies at a certain time and place in Earth's history unless God planned it. Even eight such predictions could not mathematically be computed. Those prophets came from different regions, and what they foretold were written down over a 1,400-year span of time. When Mr. Irizarry wrapped up his presentation, John Carter was nowhere to be found. **Strike three! John's out.**

From then on, his Sundays would not be spent anywhere near the building where Sunday school met. It was not the tension with his instructors that caused him to leave but rather his rejection of the truth, which he allowed to become cemented in his head and heart. Now he was going to begin to live his life his way. It would be his goal to build his own home one day. He did not understand that he had already begun to do just that.

The Jews of old had their temple (*worship home*) destroyed because of idolatry. The prophets continued to warn them as the preachers of our day do. **In the Old Testament, *Jeremiah 44:16-17* records what the backsliding Jews of that prophet's day thought about his prophetic utterances:** *"As for the word you have spoken to us in the name of the Lord, we will not listen to you! But we will certainly do whatever has gone out of our own mouth."* The saying "the more things change, the more they remain the same" will recur in this account of a person on the run from his Creator and Savior.

John Carter had been "doing his own thing" his entire life and was now about to continue his destructive path without any interference from those in church or his family. His protection was now gone. The focus of his life would be on John Carter.

Idolatry does not only mean bowing down to a wooden, stone, or metal image. Rather than being "in your face," Idolatry can manifest in a passive way. Its roots are in the curse of pride that all of us inherited from our first parents. In a broad sense, it is an attitude of "I need," "I want," "I say," "I think," "I will do," and "**I am**." Incidentally, there is only one **I AM** (*Exodus 3:14*), **and it is God Almighty!** This attitude results from our fallen nature.

While there was no indication that John had a "money addiction," or many of the other addictions we all know about. He did have an addiction to his will being done on Earth and not as it is done in Heaven. We—you and me—are not to have any other "god" before us.

There are many things that can sidetrack people and take them down a rabbit hole. There is a **big god** to watch out for, dear friends. Even poor people can be covetous. This big god is called $$$$$$$$. In the New Testament, *1 Timothy 6:9-10* tells us that love for money will bring snares, harmful lust, sorrow, and even destruction and perdition. It is in fact the root of all evil. The Apostle Paul uses such harsh language here because love of money leads to a love of the power that goes with it. Money fuels pride so that lovers of it wind up being gods unto themselves.

God is concerned for our well-being and wants us to love Him rather than things. All things pass away. You will not see a U-Haul truck going to gravesites with the stuff of the deceased so that they can enjoy their accumulated earthly things in the afterlife.

All these kinds of teachings and warnings from "that Rulebook" that John's parents went by were nonsense to John Carter because he believed that it was written to keep him in a religious box, and he wanted to be free. In fact, it irritated him that it sounded like their God, who can't even be seen, was saying it had to be His way and that He had to be the supreme commander over people's lives, or they would be on the highway to hell. The conflict was that John had set himself up as his own god and the final authority in his life.

Repeatedly, in one way or the other, it says in the Bible that God alone is God and that we are to have no other gods but Him.

Chapter Seven: Captured

John was hanging out with other misfit types but, one day, this behavior would end abruptly. That day was rapidly approaching. He and his ne'er-do-well buddies conceived a brilliant idea. Because he was a little older, his buddies looked to him as the leader of what would be another doomed venture. They decided to break into the local deli and steal only the cheese. All of them cracked up at the idea and, about one o'clock that morning, they made another poor life choice. "Thou shall not steal" is the commandment in *Exodus 20:15*, a verse that these delinquents knew but ignored.

They called themselves the Provolone Perps (perpetrators), thinking their crime to be just a funny prank. At the appointed hour, they went to the backdoor of Mike's Meat Market, which they easily forced open. One of the

Perps immediately grabbed some cheese and started to smear it along a counter as the rest laughed. Five minutes later, two police cars arrived. The two officers turned off their headlights as they drove up, parked nearby, and slowly made their way toward the deli. It seemed that one of the genius gang members had tripped a silent alarm.

A chunky 15-year-old named Charlie had his head stuffed into a chunk of smelly provolone that he had found on a shelf in the store's large fridge. As he was eating the evidence, he looked up to find an angry police officer staring at him and mumbled, "Oh no." The gravity of the situation did not sink in for John until he felt and heard the metal handcuffs click behind his back. He was no longer a kid and would be going to the criminal court as an adult. He knew that he was going to have to face the judge and, worse yet, his dad.

Walter Carter was a soft-spoken and devout Christian. It did not surprise him that John found himself standing before a judge. He himself had faced difficulties during his youth. He was a victim of child abuse and, until he became a Christian, harbored bitterness and anger toward his own father. He had been headstrong and frequently found himself

51

in trouble, usually for getting into fistfights with bullies. That's what he thought his dad was, a bully. So, fighting had been Walter's way of venting. Perhaps that is why he did not know how to balance leniency with harsher form of punishment when his middle son exhibited anti-social behavior. His confusing signals complicated his dealings with his middle boy, who was bright and knew how to "play" him.

John Carter was the way he was in school and everywhere he went. He never understood the concept of "no-no, don't touch" or when to keep his mouth shut. He was normally an easy-going young man and, like his father, soft-spoken and polite. However, when it came to doing the right thing and obeying, he opposed all voices of authority. Other kids were sneaky about not doing the right thing, but he simply thought that he knew better than those who tried to tell him what to do. Still, he knew right from wrong. This day, though he was going to have to keep his big mouth shut and would certainly not be able to "play the judge."

Chapter Eight: Unwanted Change

Walter Carter arrived in the courtroom just as the bailiff said, "All rise, the Honorable Judge James Howarth presiding." Just before his son was called for arraignment, Walter asked the bailiff for permission to briefly approach the bench. His request was granted, so he stepped forward to speak with the judge. He offered to pay the deli owner for all the damages as well as all court costs if the judge would consider offering two choices regarding his boy's punishment. Normally, this type of negotiation does not take place at the arraignment stage of a criminal court case, but the judge agreed to Walter's request when he saw his tears and distraught countenance and perceived his anxiety as a father. Walter was sad and angry and determined that, today, he would not be played.

So, when the bailiff brought John before the judge, he presented him with two options and told him to choose quickly because he had a busy calendar. John reluctantly accepted what he considered the lesser of two evils that had been offered him. He pleaded guilty to a lesser charge so he would qualify legally for his choice. The next voice of authority that John heard after his sentencing was not one that he wanted to hear, but it represented something far better than the other option, which was six years in prison.

Chapter Nine: You're in the Army Now

"Private," barked the sergeant, "I told you twenty push-ups, not nineteen! Now give me twenty more!" Though John hated military rules and regulations—especially that manual the Army went by—he somehow managed to distinguish himself. He was smart and, despite being small in stature, surpassed many other recruits in the physical training. He was competitive by nature and loved challenges. He was also a crack shot, a skill that landed him in the trenches sooner than some of the other soldiers. Several months later, he was told that he was going to be deployed, though not where his assignment would be.

One night, he was awakened by a tap on his shoulder from his sergeant. "Pack your gear, Carter." Private John Carter knew that this was the assignment he had been told about and, within an hour, was on a chopper. The flight lasted for a couple of hours, bringing him to a military airbase in the early morning. After a brief meal, he embarked on an army air transport for parts unknown. During the flight he was told he was going to Afghanistan.

Not long after arriving at his new assignment, John realized that Afghanistan with its mountainous terrain was the main hot spot in which the United States had a physical presence. As soon as he emerged from the transport, he heard his lieutenant shout, "Incoming, incoming!" followed a second later by nearby explosions and pitiable cries of pain. Calls for a medic seemed to be coming from all directions. John's platoon and other combat troops in that area were pinned down by enemy rocket and mortar fire. His orders were to dig in and hold fast until the air cover arrived and some heavy weaponry from behind the front lines. Many soldiers had been killed or injured in this combat zone. John did not like the fact they were on the defensive instead of the offensive. The enemy did have the advantages of occupying the high ground and more powerful weapons, but John reasoned within himself, *So what?*

At the command post, John was briefed about what the division was up against, where the enemy entrenchments were located, and the logistical and tactical challenges. The troops were encouraged by the news that help would be coming, though the fact that the commanders were not exactly sure when bothered John greatly.

His superiors quickly became impressed with Private Carter's ability to handle a rifle and enlisted Lieutenant Dana Lowe, a former sharpshooter and sniper, to train him to disguise himself, blend into the terrain, and, generally, how to stay alive. He soon became known as a marksman, and without a doubt the division's best shot. Many of the young soldiers looked up to him, and he loved the attention. After several weeks in which he racked up many confirmed hits, including an enemy general, somehow, John concluded that his renown meant that he was entitled to offer suggestions to his superiors and that they would be thrilled at this private's answers to their problems.

While detailed to various locations in the area, John had learned the terrain. Based on his observations, he thought that he had identified the enemy's weaknesses. Once he was convinced that he had figured out what the problem was and that he knew better than the ranking officers did about the challenges involved, he determined to explain to them how to resolve the situation favorably. In his mind, he saw that, little by little, the American soldiers were being killed while those in charge seemed just to sit back and let it happen. Eventually, he could not resist the urge to speak out any longer. No other thought or idea was acceptable to him. Just like in sports, he was going to tell his superiors, a good defense is an offense.

So, greatly encouraged by the attention that he was receiving as a sniper, John boldly approached the sergeant who was his immediate superior and shared his thoughts. He even brought some maps he'd drawn while at his sniper nests. However, the sergeant abruptly interrupted him and told him to take his post. Shocked and angered by this treatment, he left the sergeant's tent and headed to the command center a couple hundred feet away where the lieutenant was. He was toying with the idea of reporting his sergeant's rudeness and lack of ability to see the obvious.

Instead, at the command center, John reiterated to Lieutenant Ron Jones what he was convinced had to be done. Again, bringing out his maps, he explained that he could take out the enemy's rocket launchers on the left bank in a surprise attack. The lieutenant, though, sneered at him and denied the request, asking whether he had spoken to his sergeant about his idea. John explained that he had but that the sergeant had dismissed him. The lieutenant then harshly ordered him back to his assigned post. John was dismayed and discouraged that his superiors would not even give him the time of day.

The concept of the chain of command did not register with him, for he now viewed the Army like a large civilian corporation, in which upward communication is frequently lacking. He felt superior to his superiors and that they were not qualified for their rank. Bitter, he was now even more determined to prove them wrong. He considered it far better to go on the offensive in a surprise attack than to sit back and be slaughtered slowly.

Hebrews 12:15 admonishes us to "be careful that a root of bitterness does not spring up and cause trouble and defile a person" (paraphrased). Bitterness is a cancer that spreads. It consumes its victims. Many people have been destroyed by harboring hate and anger.

In typically headstrong fashion, feeling insulted, John set out to disobey the direct orders of his sergeant and lieutenant. His obstinacy became more about showing them how wrong they were than simply destroying the enemy. *Samuel 15:23b* states that "Stubbornness is as the sin of iniquity and idolatry." Stubbornness is a deep-seated sin that goes down into the fiber of a person's being, tainting and distorting their character and reasoning, and is always fostered by pride. This time, John was going to be sneaky about what he intended to do, and he was not going to waste time making his move.

Chapter Ten: A "Hero" is Born

It was a cool breezy evening; John lay awake in his bunk until all but those on watch were asleep. Arming himself to the teeth, he then snuck out of the camp without being spotted by the guards and proceeded to move uphill toward the enemy's main position. He crouched low as he advanced. Whenever he heard a noise, he hugged the ground and remained motionless on his belly. He remembered the times that he and his father had spent hunting together, moving quietly so as not to alert their quarry. Using that skill, he waited for just the right time to make his move. With the grenades and ammunition that he had "borrowed" from his camp's arsenal, this lone ranger was about to go into action.

In the New Testament, *Titus 3:1* instructs us to be subject to rulers and authorities, and *Romans 13:1-5* explains in detail why we are to obey the authorities who have been placed over us and the consequences for those who do not. None of these thoughts or concepts meant anything to Private Carter as he stealthily approached his quarry. Eventually, he drew close enough to hear the enemy soldiers talking among themselves. He took soft, shallow breaths as he waited for the opportunity to attack. When a cloud partially blocked the moonlight, he went on the offensive with the same drive with which he had tried to explain to his superiors which he considered to be unqualified and dense.

With lightning speed, he assaulted the enemy outpost. First, he took out the soldiers nearest to him. Every deadly accurate shot found its mark. He ducked back into the woods at the clearing's edge and came up behind some of the enemy soldiers and continued shooting. Using every hand grenade with equal accuracy, he engaged the enemy mercilessly. He caught the overconfident soldiers completely off guard relaxing in the camp. Some were unarmed. Before his adversaries knew what was happening, it was over, with twenty-three enemy soldiers dead or severely wounded. The camp was destroyed, including the deadly rocket launchers.

John saw nothing moving except two enemy soldiers on security patrol in the distance who were racing back to their camp in response to the gunfire and explosions. They arrived in time to fire at John as he began making his way back to the U.S. camp, and their bullets found their mark. Shot in the back, he fell to the ground but managed to roll over and fire his rifle in their direction. Despite his injuries, his marksmanship prevailed, and both fell dead.

The gunfire and explosions roused those at the U.S. camp, too. John's grenades had taken out the enemy's ammunition dump, rockets, and stored fuel, lighting up the skyline. Everything in the area seemed to be burning. The officers stationed the troops on the perimeter and prepared for an engagement should the enemy counterattack.

It took the wounded private a long time to crawl through the tall grass back to his camp. He was unaware that he had sustained other wounds during his one-man raid. Initially, the adrenaline pumping through his veins prevented him from feeling any pain. Still, he knew that he was losing a lot of blood, and soon the first surge of intense pain hit him. The adrenaline was gone. His camp seemed to be hundreds of miles away as he continued to crawl through the grass. Each time he pressed down on his elbows, a searing pain shot up his back and through his chest.

At one point, he turned his head to see whether any enemy soldiers were behind him, and what he saw puzzled his foggy mind. Amid the bright fiery yellow and red flames that were illuminating the dark background of the night, he saw two bright white lights. They did not seem to be part of the flaming destruction but rather like illuminated clouds. He turned his head and continued to move slowly forward, resolved to stay focused, though his body and mind were weakening rapidly.

The windy season had come to the region a few weeks previously, and the gusts that night were particularly strong. Sparks from the cascading fires were spraying in every direction. The embers from the trees and grass began to ignite everything that could burn, including the trees and grass around John. Thick, dark clouds of acrid smoke filled the air, making it hard for him to take a breath. He was still moving in the right direction but painfully slowly. With fierce determination, he pressed on, knowing that a painful death awaited him if he could not make it back to the camp. Each time that he coughed, he was instantly reminded of the serious wounds that he had received, but somehow the agony kept him from passing out. *I am going to make it,* he said over and over to himself.

All the soldiers, including the brass, were furiously digging trenches in an effort to impede the approaching firestorm. They were no longer concerned about the enemy attacking since they believed that nothing could make it through the approaching wall of flames alive. Their ammunition lockers were safe at another location.

When John heard the voices of some U.S. soldiers, he called out in a labored voice and raised his arm in the hope that someone would notice him. The crackling flames were almost upon him when a soldier peering through the flames and smoke spotted him and called out to a couple of others, "Someone's coming out of the fire!" They ran toward him and, amid the smoke, snatched him from the flames that had just begun licking at his boots. All three were screaming, "Medic, medic! Over here!"

Chapter Eleven: A Rebel with a Good Aim

John had done the nearly impossible, and word of his feat quickly spread among the troops and officers alike. The general in command of the division responded to the news by calling an emergency staff meeting, where he told his officers that he had a problem and needed suggestions for handling it. He explained that a certain Private John Carter had blatantly disobeyed a direct order on two occasions and had done so in a defiant manner that could not be reconciled with the Army's rules of order. He had stolen supplies and violated several other ordinances.

The Army could not safely operate if such conduct became rampant. Lack of discipline would invite disaster among the ranks. Already, Carter's incredibly brave (or stupid) one-man-show was being talked about by the troops the general further explained. He was thought to be a hero, and they wanted to be brave just like him. Disorder breeds chaos. By contrast, the Lord is an orderly God; thus, *1 Samuel 15:22* says that "obedience is better than sacrifice."

A seasoned captain responded that the private's action had, after all, made it possible for the division to move against the enemy from that unprotected left flank. Ultimately, because of what Carter had done, the U.S. force was able to take positions above the enemy encampments and quickly outflank and destroy all the remaining forces that had been hidden from attack, reducing the deadly mortars to rubble and taking many prisoners. The U.S. casualties had been minimal. Eventually, through a coordinated assault, the U.S. force secured the entire territory. The general, though, was shaking his head back and forth as he listened, and he replied, "I already am aware of that, gentlemen, but that is not why we are here."

Then a major made a comment that angered the general, pointing out that Private Carter had only been in the Army a short while and was new to the ways of the service. When he saw the general's countenance, the major quickly added that this was not an excuse. The general retorted, "This soldier did, in fact, know that what he did was wrong just as sure as he knew that what he was doing as a sniper was right. He knew what our manual says. The fact that what he did was far above the line of duty can't be denied. However, that doesn't make him a hero but rather a rebel with a good aim." Additionally, the incident had somehow reached the media, and ultimately, Carter would be looked upon as a brave soldier who had nearly died for his country. The private's growing celebrity status had been the general's main reason for calling this high-level meeting.

The solution to the dilemma became apparent when a lieutenant spoke up and informed the general that Carter's wounds were severe enough to prevent him from returning to active service. Accordingly, they decided that, instead of giving him a bad conduct discharge for insubordination, they would sever him from the Army with a medical discharge and give him the Silver Star. The general ended the meeting by telling his subordinates, "I believe that this young man's future will prove to be problematic, and his life is likely ruined unless he makes some significant changes." He had no idea how prophetic his words were.

Chapter Twelve: A Visitation, No Change

The army medics could only do so much to help Carter because his wounds were so severe. They did not have the equipment or skills to perform the series of operations that were required on the spot. The staff did what they could, stabilizing the severely wounded in preparation for surgery elsewhere, but the capabilities of the makeshift on-site hospital were limited. The wounds of many were too severe for treatment there. Carter was among the severely injured. Even the pain medicine did not take full effect among the wounded.

For the second time in his life, John was laid up with a high fever. This time, it came and went, causing great concern for the medical team. After he had spent three days lying on a hard mattress in the infirmary, a medical chopper arrived to take John and several other critically injured soldiers to the mainland where they would be operated on. Eventually, they would be flown home to complete their recovery. Some did not make it.

When John finally arrived at an Army hospital in the States, he was still weak and experiencing severe pain. One night, after tossing and turning, he sat up, sensing that he was not alone in his room. He heard a soft, high-pitched giggling from the far side of the room and smelled a putrid odor from that direction. Straining to see in the dark, he was sure that he glimpsed a shadowy figure pointing at him and whispering "Mine, all mine! Hee-hee-hee!" A cold chill ran up his spine, but sleep overcame him. This was now his third encounter with death, and it was not the last time he saw that dark figure and heard its cackling taunts.

The base chaplain, Captain Shawn McCracken, visited several times. On one occasion, he said, "You know, John, you had a mighty close call in those mountains. Surely you don't think, with the odds stacked against you, that it was only your marksmanship and luck that got you out alive, do you?"

John didn't want to engage in a religious discussion and simply replied, "Who knows for sure, chaplain? I just want to get out of here and start my life over again."

The chaplain could see that John was not open to a serious talk about what starting over actually meant. When he left the hospital, he called his parents and told them about his attempts to minister to their son and an idea that had occurred to him. He offered his diagnosis of their son's spiritual condition, and they accepted it and said that they would follow through in trying to help him in this regard. Chaplain Shawn believed that there was a call on their son's life but that he was resisting it. He told them that he would put his name on a prayer list that he kept for servicemen and women and suggested that they do the same, and they agreed to do so.

During John's four-month stay in the hospital and rehab, he talked often with his family. He loved to hear from all of them. His brothers considered him a hero. Many in their hometown had heard about his incredible feats in combat.

One day, his brother Kevin called and said in a worried and odd tone, "John, are you really alright? I mean, really?"

"Sure, Kev," John responded, "I'm fine, I'm fine." He knew that his big brother wasn't talking about his physical injuries because, when Kevin prayed for him before hanging up, there was no mention of his wounds or when he was going to get out of the hospital.

How many times, when we call or see people and ask how they are doing, they respond with the same "I'm fine; I'm okay," and we know in our gut that they are not okay. One thing is for sure: sending someone a text with the letters RUOK will never reveal anything. This is such a useless and dead form of communication in our rush-rush, flippant society.

John's parents still had strong reservations about him because they could hear the tone of his heart as he spoke. *Proverbs: 4:23* says, "Keep [that is, guard] your heart with all diligence; for out of it spring the issues of life." *Matthew 12:34* says, "From out of the abundance of the heart, the mouth speaks." John's parents would listen intently, but what they heard coming from the mouth of their son told them that nothing significant had changed in him. He openly called his superiors morons and other derogatory names. He bragged about "taking the bull by the horns" to show his superiors that he was right, and they were wrong.

When he left the rehabilitation facility, he was minus one kidney and a couple of ribs. He received the Silver Star in a short ceremony and left the service with a medical discharge. He was now free to do what he had always wanted to do, with no more stringent rules to follow. Finally, he was going to be his own man. He wouldn't return home as many wounded servicemen did. He was going to go it alone, without interference from anyone, and that included his family. For all intents and purposes, he was now just a lone shadow among many other phantoms in a crowd.

Chapter Thirteen: John the Builder

John's life's dream was to build his own home exactly the way he wanted it. Unknown to him, as we have seen, the groundwork for that dream had been laid years ago. Now, John found a piece of property in the lowlands. There was a dirty river nearby that ran slowly past the backyard. The main road was a quarter mile away, so it wouldn't be difficult to bring in supplies. The project began in the fall. It was a disaster from beginning to end.

John didn't consult a construction manual or seek any ideas, advice, or counsel from those who had successfully built their own homes. *Proverbs 11:14* says "Where there is no counsel, the people fall, but in the multitude of counsel is safety." Another translation reads "the people will be defeated." Tragically, over time, that truth would become real to John as he was nearing his life-or-death encounter with the Prince of Darkness.

The roof construction was shoddy, so John did not have the protective covering from above for his home. In the basement, he didn't use the supports required to undergird a home. The foundation that he laid was of lesser quality than the building code required. In fact, he didn't even lay the footing on solid ground. He laid it on sandy soil that was prone to shift.

There is a scripture that applies directly to the foundation that John laid. In *Matthew 7:24-27,* Jesus says,

"Therefore, whoever hears these sayings of Mine and does them, I will liken him to a wise man who built his house on the rock; and the rains descended, and the floods came, and the winds blew and beat on that house; and it did not fall, for it was founded on the rock. But everyone that hears these sayings of Mine and does not do them will be like a foolish man who built his house on the sand and, when the rain descended, the floods came, and the winds blew and beat on the house, it fell. And great was its fall."

The same could be said for the walls, plumbing, and electricity. All the materials that John used to build his home were low-grade or of inferior quality. Consequently, there was no way he could safely function in his abode. Still, he liked what he saw.

The work done by this 'construction expert' originated in his own imagination and faulty reasoning. *Romans 12:2* talks about how the mind needs to be transformed and renewed to correct a person's thinking: "And do not be conformed to this world but be transformed by the renewing of your mind." Even a dose of common sense would have prevailed, but not for this blockhead. There is an old saying about someone beating his head against the wall, that it will feel so good when he stops. There is another adage that, tells us when a person does the same thing over and over and expects different results, it is the definition of insanity.

John's construction project was difficult and took years to complete but, in the end, he got what he wanted: he did it his way.

Chapter Fourteen: His Dream Comes True

John was happy because he was encouraged by like-minded friends. They were kindred spirits because their hearts were just as messed up as his was. He was finally a homeowner and was grateful for their support and counsel, and they became frequent party guests at his rickety residence. *Psalm 1:1* speaks of those kinds of friends and comes with a blessing for those who do not follow their counsel. *Proverbs 13:20* puts it this way: "He who walks with wise men will be wise, but a companion of fools will be destroyed." That truth is not just for the character in this story. It is one of the axioms of the ages that has endured time when applied to the choices that people make in picking their friends. Do they make their decisions based on sound judgment, or do they give way to the foolhardy suggestions and ways of those whom they call friends? Our social media of today is a great reference point for this truth.

Ultimately, though, John's plan came with a huge price tag. Slowly, over a very long period of time he began to realize that he had no inner peace and no lasting joy or happiness. The jokes that they told and fun that he had drinking with his sick friends had faded into stale meaningless memories. He sensed on the inside that something was wrong or missing.

This know-it-all guy was not aware that a lack of inner peace and joy is always a sign that something is not right on the inside. In *John 14:27,* Jesus says, "Peace I leave with you, my peace I give to you; not as the world gives do I give to you. Let not your heart be troubled, neither let it be afraid." John's heart was troubled, and soon he would know real fear.

The pseudo-master builder knew that he was messed up and needed help, but, unfortunately, he had become comfortable in the wreck of a structure that he had built and did not possess the power or desire, [which is defined as the grace of God,] to see a meaningful change on the inside of his heart's home. That is why the exterior of his home was showing signs of wear and seemed to be slowly starting to decay and crumble. What he did not know was how quickly things would fall apart. His heart's house would indeed fall. It would, in fact, be destroyed.

When John heard about the violent death of his friend Bob Anderson, it really shook him up. While he himself was not religious, at times he did wonder about the "so-called" afterlife. This was one of those times. Bob had died in a bar fight, and John knew that he was a wacky dude who did not believe in anything but himself. He wondered at that point whether there is a God and whether heaven and hell are real. *If so, where is Bob now? Surely, there is a right and wrong,* he thought.

In an intimate moment, a time to pause and reflect, John also recalled to mind the death of Tommy and of his soldier friends. He just shook his head because he had no answers to his thoughts or questions. It was the beginning of a soul-searching time for him, but time was running out for this lost soul, and he would again encounter death.

Chapter Fifteen: Deep Reflections

As the sole owner of his dilapidated residence, John began to reminisce about the car accident that he had survived against the odds and how his friend Tommy had not. Over and over, he pondered over his near-death experiences when he was younger. John remembered the pitchfork incident and again shook his head. He wondered about the time that he had seen, in a dream or vision, ugly beasts crouching, and other beings dressed in white with their arms raised high. And what were those bright lights that he saw on the burning mountain top? John was no longer sure what he believed about death and the hereafter. He was no longer sure that he had "lucked out." He remembered the night in the hospital when he had seen a shadowy figure in the far corner of his room and heard it giggling. That memory made him extremely uncomfortable, and he started shivering.

John expressed his concern about Bob to his buddies. Lying Larry was no help. Neither was Miserable Mike, Sarcastic Sam, nor any of his other flaky friends. In the Old Testament, *Isaiah 48:22* states "'There is no peace, says the Lord, for the wicked." In his confusion, John began thinking back to his childhood days, trying to remember some meaningful things that his dad had taught him or that he had heard in Sunday school. Partial thoughts would begin to surface only to quickly fade away. Even the memories of joy-filled times with his family only added to his pain and sadness. He was feeling empty and alone.

Psalm 34:11-22 is extremely pertinent regarding John's plight. It gives so much sound insight into a person's life. If John had read and taken to heart those verses, instead of being confused, he would have been convinced that the Bible is a book for all people, including him. It speaks of our deliverance from fear and trouble and how near God is to the brokenhearted. That psalm assures those who are righteous that they will be heard by the Lord. He will redeem the souls of those who trust Him. It also warns that those who hate the righteous will be cut off from God and destroyed.

The Word of God covers every circumstance during all the seasons of a person's life. There is an age-old saying that says, "The more things change, the more they remain the same." That is what makes the Holy Scriptures the most up-to-date and relevant book ever written. "There is nothing new under the sun," *Ecclesiastes 1:9*. God's Word is timeless because He is timeless.

"In the beginning, GOD...." It all began with Him. It will end with Him, too. As previously stated, one of His names is "**I AM**"—not, "I Once Was" or "I Hope to Be." He is eternal and always in the present. He is "**the alpha and omega, the beginning and the end**" (*Revelations 21:6*). This mighty Warrior and Lover of our souls is in the midst of our sorrows and pain.

Zephaniah 3:17 states, "The Lord your God in your midst, the Mighty One, will save you; He will rejoice over you with gladness, He will quiet you with His love, he will rejoice over you with singing."

John did not know that he was not alone. He also was unaware that the Lord was calling him or even that he had been running from Him. The battle raging in his heart and mind was for his soul. His shallow thinking was only on the fact that he was miserable, but God was at work and would again show him his power and love.

A week or so after Bob's death, John was having a restless night's sleep when, suddenly, he felt a presence all around him. He was not sure whether he was having a dream, but it seemed very real. He opened his eyes. What he saw amazed him, but he was not frightened. In his room, he was looking at the same type of lights that he had seen when he was wounded and crawling through the mountainside grass and had turned his head to see whether the enemy was following him. There were two of them, and they were standing a few feet in front of him. They were not as bright as before and much smaller. It looked as if their clothes were made of a soft glowing light, and they appeared to have a human shape.

Both had their arms raised high the way he remembered people in the church did when they were praising God. Nothing was said, but John was overwhelmed with a peace that was coming from their presence. Once again, sleep overcame him.

Scriptures such *John 14:27*, where Jesus says, "Peace, I leave you, my peace I give unto you," need to be repeated, for we all want that "Peace that passes all our understanding, for it will guard and keep our hearts and minds in Christ Jesus" (*Philippians 4:7*, paraphrased).

Often, we are forgetful hearers, especially if we are going through stuff. To know the Prince of Peace and to call upon Him during those times will make all the difference regarding our gaining the victory, as opposed to dwelling over and over on the negativity involved in a dismal situation.

Our war hero still did not grasp the fact that God's angels were present in his room and that they were there to strengthen him for his coming life-or-death battle with the Prince of Darkness. The God of Peace was trying once again to reach out to him before it was too late. John Carter was affected by the quiet serenity associated with the vision. It was the opposite of how he had been feeling lately. He remained clueless about how close he was to missing his eternal destiny.

Chapter Sixteen: The Encounter Begins

One day, a handsome elderly gentleman knocked on the door of the dilapidated home, where John and several of his friends were partying. This man had bright eyes, a nice countenance, and was dressed immaculately. John invited the stranger to join the gathering. Almost immediately, the elderly man began to offer "sound reasoning" to the owner and his guests. He told them that they were all good people and that they should not be concerned about what the townspeople said regarding their wild, drunken escapades.

Over and over, he reiterated that no one was perfect and that no one had a right to judge them. He particularly warned them about religious people who wanted to "get into their heads" by threatening them with damnation or eternal suffering. John's friends were mesmerized by this stranger. He advised them to look after self (me, myself, and I) by recounting an old saying, "If you have a friend who is tried and true, you sink him before he drowns you." Though what he told them was absurd and hardly sound reasoning, his audience loved it. Everyone was awestruck by his commanding presence and smooth voice. Every time he spoke, the guests wanted to hear more because he spoke with the deep voice of authority. *2 Corinthians 11:14-15* should have warned them not to consider or be taken off guard by how good a person looks or what they say because "Satan himself transforms himself into an angel of light, and his ministers can also transform themselves into ministers of righteousness."

When this guest saw John trying to bring up some of the things that he could remember from his childhood and how they differed from the so-called advice this "father figure" offered, the old gentleman mocked and laughed at him. John's friends dutifully followed suit. John had now become quite distraught, and nothing could comfort him. He was convinced that, somehow, he had taken a wrong turn in his life and that his home was in shambles.

Regarding a critical element of the Christian faith, Paul says in *2 Corinthians 7:10*, "For godly sorrow produces repentance leading to salvation not to be regretted, but the sorrow of the world leads to death." That is where the sorrow of some does not come with the faith that would produce a change in their hearts and lives.

When the stranger saw that his laughter and persuasive words could not make John think in the way in which he wanted, he turned against him. He began to accuse him of things that he was, in fact, guilty of. Speaking with great confidence and power, he even brought religion into his arguments. In an effort to frighten the battered homeowner and win him over to his side, the elderly man quoted such Bible verses as "The soul that sins shall surely die" and "The wages of sin is death." He told John that he had violated every one of the Ten Commandments and deserved God's wrath and eternal judgment. John, staring into the dark beady eyes of this man, felt strength draining from within. New Testament book of *Romans chapter 6* verse *23*, which the stranger had just quoted, bore witness to John's wayward life. Amid all the condemnation being heaped on the builder, his tormenter was careful not to include the last part of

Romans 6:23, "But the gift of God is eternal life in Christ Jesus our Lord."

People never receive "the whole truth and nothing but the truth" when they are accused by the devil, his followers, or so-called friends. They will always mix truth with error. It takes discernment to separate the two. A little lie is still a lie, and it can disguise itself as the real deal.

This once arrogant builder, who wanted to go it alone, now realized that he had no shielding from above, for, as we have seen, none was built into the fabric of his inner home. The relentless onslaught from the man whom he had personally invited into his home continued. Now John's deflated ego left him with no strength in his body, mind, or spirit. In his frightened condition, this once brave soldier cowered before his accuser. He was unaware that "God was his strength and his shield" (*Psalm 28:7,* paraphrased). He also did not know that "another One" was nearby and watching the pitiful scene unfold. God promises to be our shield and strength, as stated in *Psalm 18:1-3.*

Chapter Seventeen: The Encounter Continues

The next night, while he was sitting alone in his shack, the elderly "man" suddenly burst into the house unannounced. When John turned, he saw a hideous being dressed all in black with a black hood partially covering his face. One protruding blood-red eye glared at him from a sickening gray and wrinkled face. John began gasping for air. The body of this once strikingly attractive houseguest had become horribly distorted. Despite the changes in the "man's" face and body, John recognized him, and he was so frightened that he almost passed out. He felt as if his life were being choked out.

John didn't know that the Bible in many places mentions that we are not to fear. Because he was not part of the flock of God, he had nothing to hold on to during this overwhelming attack. As John the Apostle says in *1 John*

4:18, "There is no fear in love; but perfect love casts out fear, because fear involves torment." This is what our crushed friend was experiencing. He did not have the love of God in his heart, and now he was being tormented.

Conversely, when a Christian becomes afraid, the admonishment is soft because it comes from his Father's love for him. These words are extremely comforting. *Luke 12:32* says, "Do not fear, little flock; it is your Father's good pleasure to give you the kingdom." These words need to be repeated because, if we dwell on our sins, we might at that point find God's promises hard to believe, because we would be running on feelings and not facts. That is where our faith comes in.

In the gnarled hand of the hideous intruder was an object that looked like a sickle. It was made of metal and wood. The putrid odor coming from him was that of something that had died and was decaying in a shallow open grave. With crooked teeth bared, he snarled and told John that God hated him and had given up on him long ago. Now he belonged to him. Then he said that he would be coming for John at the stroke of midnight on the following night. As he was leaving, he began giggling and, in a high-pitched cackle, repeated in a taunting sing-song voice, "You're mine, you're mine, you are all mine, jerk. Tee-hee-hee."

At that point, John realized that this was the same shadowy creature he had seen in the corner of his room in the hospital. This was now his fourth encounter with death. The difference was that now he had met its author. He suddenly realized that the Prince of Darkness, also known as the Prince of Death, was real and that Satan had been after his soul for his whole life.

Clutching his gut in physical pain, he was now more broken than his house. He was beyond consoling, for the deep dread of death and hell had gripped him. Regarding the subject of hell, the Bible speaking about Jesus says in *Hebrews 2: 14-15,* "That through His death He would destroy him who had the power of death, that is the devil, and release those who through the fear of death were held in bondage all their lives." John's ignorance of that promise was his own doing. He was shaking violently and could not stop his body from convulsing. He began to cry, but even that was hard to do as the air would quickly leave him and cause a gasping mixed with a muffled groaning.

If John Carter was a believer and had known and believed what John the Apostle had said, he would have understood why he was so terrified and could have relied on *John 10:10-11* for comfort. In those powerful verses Jesus said, "The thief [Satan] comes to steal, kill, and to destroy, but I have come that they may have life and have it more abundantly. I am the good shepherd. The good shepherd gives His life for the sheep."

Can you see the Authority of the Christ presented in *Hebrews 2: 14-15 and in John 10: 10-11?* He has the power to destroy the devil and the power of death and to release the prisoners from fear, as well as give to give us His abundant life. This all came about because He was on an incredible rescue mission and was willing and able to do what we could not. This is the good news. The good shepherd gave his life for the sheep.

Chapter Eighteen: Broken at Last

When the twisted one left, John was in a state of total panic and collapsed on the floor. He attempted to pray for the first time in his life, but the gates of Heaven were like brass bars to him. He tried to remember what he had heard as a young boy when he used to go to church, but to no avail. It had something to do with mercy, forgiveness, and God's love, but he could not put it together. Oh, how he missed his family and how his parents loved him and tried to show him the right way to go. Over and over, he cried out within himself, *Oh mom, oh dad!* Oh, how he had mocked his Bible teachers. He was in tears and could hardly speak. His life was now destroyed by the destroyer. He had played into his dreadful hands.

John did remember that God was holy and just in all His ways and must judge sin. And, yes, he was as guilty as sin itself. But the Word of God reveals that all Earth's people are sinners. As mentioned, it is in God's providence and mercy to forgive us. He put all our crimes and offenses against His righteousness on His Holy Son so that we could stand before Him as people who are totally redeemed. Jesus took the judgment (the stroke) that was due us and died in our place. That part of God's plan John had either forgotten or never believed. Rescue and redemption have always been the central theme of the Bible.

John 3:16 says, **"For God so loved the world that He gave His only begotten son, that whosoever believes in Him should not perish but have eternal life."** That well-known verse would have given this builder hope in his desperate hour of need, but again he did not know the Bible (note, please, verses *14-21*). Many Bible verses speak of God's mercy, grace, love, forgiveness, and restoration. Sad to say, many people like John do not know how they can make peace with their Maker. Also, sad to say, some do not even care about such things.

Slowly, in his exhausted mind, John recalled some words from two old hymns. One was "Jesus loves me, this I know, for the Bible tells me so," and the other was "He walks with

me, and He talks with me, and He tells me I am His own."
Oh, the comfort that this broken sinner would have received
if only he had believed *Isaiah 44:22*. It could not be any
plainer. It was written to the Jews but is for everyone who is
a believer in the Jewish Messiah, Jesus the Christ. This verse
clearly states, "I have blotted out like a thick cloud your
transgressions, and, like a thick cloud, your sins. Return to
me, for I have redeemed you."

Other verses speak in a similar manner to those who want
to have their heart's home cleansed and find forgiveness.
Yes, it is always on God's terms. No human, including John
Carter, could bargain with Him. Listen to the foundational
facts that are recorded in the New Testament, in *Acts 3:19-
20*, "Repent therefore and be converted, that your sins may
be blotted out, so that the times of refreshing may come from
the presence of the Lord, and that He may send Jesus Christ
who was before preached unto you." These verses are a
prerequisite for and central to making peace with God the
Father. John had never done the only reasonable thing that he
could have done, considering what it cost the King of Kings
in terms of His suffering and dying in John's place.

John Carter had not cared that Jesus rose victoriously from the grave. This fact had no personal meaning to him. The Lord had freely taken all his sins and guilt, along with all the associated shame, and, in effect, erased all of John's culpability from the Father's book of records. John, however, had rejected the Savior and is not the only one to dismiss the message of the Gospel (the Good News).

A great and noble gift has been given to mankind, and that gift can never be earned or bought. It has already been bought and paid for by the Lord Jesus Christ in the shedding His blood for us on Mount Calvary. Our good works cannot add to that. Works of love follow from that fact. *1 John 4:10-11* states, "In this is love, not that we loved God, but that He loved us and sent His Son to be the propitiation [i.e., to make full payment] for our sins. Beloved, if God so loved us, we also ought to love one another."

In great fear, John kept praying the words of those songs all night long and into the evening of the "day of reckoning." Nothing seemed to help except the words "He loves me" and

"I am His own." Still, he felt so empty. He was desperately afraid and could not stop trembling.

In sorrow, after going it alone for his whole life, he began to weep bitter tears. He was not aware of the many Bible verses that offer help and comfort. Most appropriate to such an occasion is *2 Kings 20:5b*. It speaks of God hearing our prayers and seeing our tears and promising to heal us. He was about to find out what *Luke 12:32* says: "Do not fear, little flock; it is your Father's good pleasure to give you the kingdom."

John also did not know that his sincere crying out had initiated an encounter with the living God. In this dark moment of his life, he was, in fact, in the presence of the Father of light and love. He was finally answering the "call of God." God was about to go to work for this broken guy.

Psalm 51:1-17 is a prayer of repentance by King David that concludes, "The sacrifices of God are a broken spirit, a broken and contrite heart. These, O God, You will not despise." All these verses become real only when we give our hearts to Jesus. All who open their hearts to God Almighty will receive His mercy. There are many verses that speak about how God listens to those who humble themselves. To the proud, He will always remain far off, as stated in *Psalm 138:6* and many other places in His Word.

Chapter Nineteen: A New Man is Born

At 11:59 that night, a soft knock sounded on John's front door. Though our homeowner was exhausted and engulfed in fear that his hour had come, a tiny bit of courage somehow welled up from within, and he opened the door a crack. Jesus had simply knocked on the door of this broken-hearted soul. God would not barge in and threaten. He is a gentleman and had been waiting for John to invite Him in so that He could speak softly to him and be the only answer to his aching, fear-driven, and sinful heart.

Standing there was a Man with a glowing countenance and a soft smile on His face. The light coming from His eyes was radiant and beautiful. In *John 12:46,* Jesus, speaking about Himself, states, "I have come as a light into the world, that whoever believes in Me should not abide in darkness." "Abide in" means to live in.

The Stranger was dressed in a shining white robe bound in the middle with a golden sash. With a nail-pierced hand, He reached out to the startled, downtrodden man and beckoned him to come with Him. *Matthew 11:28* says, "Come unto Me, all you who labor and are heavy-laden [because of being weighed down by sin and wrong choices], and I will give you rest."

John's heart paused for a second, and then, in desperation and hope, he flung open the door and grabbed the Stranger's hand. Though he did not know what was happening or where this Stranger would take him, he trusted Him and went with Him.

Proverbs 3:5-8 tells us, "Trust in the Lord with all of our heart and lean not on your own understanding; in all your ways, acknowledge Him, and He shall direct our steps." The passage goes on to say, "Do not be wise in your own eyes [that is, conceited]; fear the Lord and depart from evil. It will be health to your flesh and strength to your bones."

As they were leaving, a shadowy figure slowly emerged from the nearby trees. When the figure saw that the Man in white had the former owner of the wrecked lodging by the hand, he shrieked in fear and fled the scene with curses falling from his lips.

Yes, the broken builder went with the Stranger that evening. He finally let the Master Carpenter begin to build his life's home over again—His way, this time. When John turned and looked back, he saw that his shack of a home had fallen apart and crumbled into the stream's murky waters. His "friends" and that tormentor were gone. He now had a new heart's home and a new destiny. Yes, his life was destroyed, but that was a good and necessary thing because now he was a new creation in Christ Jesus and a new life had begun. *2 Corinthians 5-17* **declares, "Therefore, if anyone is in Christ, he is a new creation; old things have passed away; behold, all things have become new."** He finally realized that the truth that God recorded in *Jeremiah 31:3* was also for him: "The LORD has appeared of old to me, saying, "Yes, I have loved you with an everlasting love; therefore, with loving kindness I have drawn you."

The place that Jesus took John Carter on that night cannot be adequately described. The beauty of the various colors and the fact that everything was alive along with the incredibly sweet perfume-like fragrances were far beyond what we who are living on this fallen planet could ever grasp. The plants and flowers were transparent, yet their various colors could be seen clearly. They seemed to be slowly swaying and bowing. There was pure peace and an absolute overpowering Love that flowed from a Great White Throne. The figure on the throne was veiled in light, and His form could not be seen. All the myriad of people had the same type of garments of light and likeness to the One who had taken him by the hand. They all had crowns on their heads, but each seemed distinct. John knew that the Stranger was Jesus the Christ, the Magnificent Son of God and the promised Savior. The sweetness of the heavenly music was so glorious and overpowering that, again, John's breath was taken away—but, this time, he did not need to breathe, for the fresh air of heaven continuously filled his entire being.

Amid the warnings, and symbolism given to us in the New Testament book of Revelations, *Revelations 21* describes **God's beautiful home.** The author of this book has attempted, in some small way, to describe what happened to John when Jesus took him by the hand from his pitiful self-made shack by putting some of that incredible scene into poetic verse. Again, even that attempt misses the true beauty that awaits His children when it is time for us to leave our temporary abode here on Earth.

He Danced with Me

Just as I am, I make no plea,

O come, Lord Jesus; dance with me.

He nodded and smiled while taking my hand,

And led me to a meadow in a faraway land.

Through the twilight hours and into the day,

He held all of my being, all of my sway.

The music of heaven long last is mine,

The dance of delight raptured in time.

The majesty of the moment forever takes hold,

As gently He guides me into His fold.

No more to fear, no more to roam,

His pastures of pleasure now are my home.

Yes, nearer than my breath He will always be,

It is Christ now in me that others must see.

Chapter Twenty: God's Protection and Provision

John Carter knew that there would be temptations within, challenges all about, and failures at times. He was aware that those old friends and that tormentor would still be lurking around. But he also knew that the One who had saved him had proved that He was the God of Love. Jesus had unshackled him from his personal prison and would now guide him through the rest of his life. God promised to care for him. Listen again to *Isaiah 46:4*: **"I will be your God through all your lifetime; I made you and I will care for you."**

He does not show favoritism. What He did for our fictional character in this encounter He is willing to do for real flesh-and-blood people. He wants to reveal Himself to anyone who will sincerely call on Him by faith—not blind faith, but faith built on the facts presented in the Bible. He is the only One who can redeem us because He paid the highest ransom for us by shedding His Holy blood for an unholy race of people. Not only that, but He also calls His people by His name. What a privilege. We are not talking about a fictional character here. He is the Living God.

As for those tests, trials, tribulations, and temptations that John would encounter, he is not alone. *1 Corinthians 10:13* records that they are common to all men and women but, because of the faithfulness of God, no Christian needs to be overpowered by the missiles and darts of temptation that the devil hurls at them. Elijah was a great and mighty prophet who lived back in Old Testament times. The Bible records this about him in *James 5:17*: "He was a man of like passion as we are." Christians do not need to fall under the influence of the world's ways and sway or to let the sinful nature with which they were born pull them down. Indeed, "The Lord Himself will provide a way of escape so we can bear it" (*1 Corinthians 10:13*, paraphrased).

God has given all His children special armament to defend them against any attack of the enemy. That is why His children are called His soldiers. Some of His chosen ones will do battle in a war somewhere and may need to endure the same type of missiles that John, our builder friend, had to endure. Others will not. But be assured all of us are in a war. The weapons and armament described in the next few paragraphs, though, are supernatural and provided by God.

Ephesians 6:10-18 gives us a complete list of the armor needed to protect us from the flaming missiles hurled at us by the devil. Friends, that armor covers us from head to toe and comes with a mighty weapon to be used offensively against the devil. It is called the Sword of the Spirit, which is the Word of God. I trust that you will read those verses and put that armor on.

"The weapons of our warfare are not made by mere man but are mighty through God to the pulling down of strongholds, casting down arguments and everything that exalts itself against the knowledge of God." The authority for that assertion is *2 Corinthians 10:2-5.*

What a weapon *agape* love is. It is a godly love that only knows how to give. It never takes for itself. It is a love that never fails. Jesus is the Creator and Author of *agape* love, and He never fails. No matter what happens we have the anchor of God's love to protect us.

In our day-to-day living, there will be insults, prejudice, lust, anger, cancer, sickness, unfairness, and a host of other ailments, challenges, and temptations with which we are all very familiar. Without that armor on, we are sitting ducks for the one who has hated God from the beginning and hates God's created human beings. He is the avowed enemy of all mankind—that's **you** and **me,** my friends. He is slick and often hides in the shadows to escape notice.

God would not have given us all these weapons if there were not going to be skirmishes on the blue planet. Expect them in the family, too. It did not take long after sin came into our world and into the heart of man that it reared its ugly head in the family. Adam and Eve's son murdered his brother. The war was on.

How could anyone not believe that there is something wrong with the people of Earth. Yes, we were created in God's image, but our image became clouded and distorted by sin. We, as Christians, daily need His armorment on and His weapons of warfare at the ready.

God did not leave us alone down here. He also gave us Christian friends to love and help us. *Psalm 91:1-16* says, "He is our refuge and shield, and His angels will guide and protect us. He will deliver and honor His people" (paraphrased). WHY? Because these privileges and blessings come to those who "love Him and have called on Him in times of trouble."

Chapter Twenty-One: Opportunities and Challenges

2 Corinthians 5:17-6:2 speaks to the results of the Gospel message taking root and going beyond that initial encounter with the Lord that results in a person joining the family of God (and becoming a new creation in Christ). This passage also states that saved people are ambassadors for Christ and represent Him wherever they go. God gives His people opportunities to share the great things that He has done for them. These one-on-one encounters with those he places in front of us are all part of our being His soldiers, His ambassadors, and His sons and daughters.

Every Christian will have opportunities to serve Him in that capacity and in many other ways. That is why a victorious Christian has the Holy Spirit flowing from within.

He will guide, empower, and protect the believers on their pilgrimage toward their final **home**, HIS HOME.

Phrase it any way you want—John Carter had been dancing with the devil his whole life, and he finally ran out of time. What about you, my friends? Time is not on your side. You do not have to be a bad person to be far from God and on the "endangered species" list. Just politely avoid His nudging and continue to build your inner home and your destiny your way.

You might feel safe in the home that you are erecting because you have never been involved in deep, dark sin as some people have. Outwardly, your heart's home might look squeaky clean. Maybe you are a church-going man, woman, or young person. You simply may not realize that you, too, might be bound and imprisoned by a me-myself-and-I attitude or habit, and are having close encounters with the Prince of Darkness as you go about your daily business.

A litmus test can help you here. Take a deep look into the mirror of your heart—even stand in front of a mirror during the test. Ask yourself honestly whether you know for sure that you are right with your Creator and that, when you die,

111

God will allow you admittance into His Eternal Home. Then ask this question: why should He accept you into His home? If you say that He should because you are not that bad of a person, or that you don't hurt people, or that you love to help people, then I urge you to continue to read this little booklet of hope to the end because a careful read will reveal that the author had you in mind when it was written.

I promise you this, dear friend: if you do read this booklet to the end, you will not only know whether you are in the right relationship with your Creator, but you will also know how to find your way home if you are not in true fellowship with the One who loves you so. That promise is directly from Him.

Chapter Twenty-Two: History Past/History Present

Adam and Eve were as close to God as one can get. Their physical home was handcrafted by God. It was a piece of heaven on earth. Their heart's *home* was pure. They walked with and talked with God in Eden's beautiful garden. However, Satan seduced and ensnared them with his lies. He convinced them that they would not die if they ate the forbidden fruit. That ruse prepared them to be won over to his side. He also convinced them that they could be like God. Believing that lie is what caused them to forsake the right way. After their encounter with the Prince of Darkness, they no longer wanted to be under God's authority, for they had become an authority unto themselves. God gave them a chance to repent, but they did not.

That sin—wanting to be like God—is why Satan was kicked out of heaven and why he used that ploy on our first parents. They fell for it and rebelled against their Creator. That choice forever altered all of humanity. Though we are created by God, we are the spiritual children of Adam and suffer from a strong desire to follow the dictates of our hearts. Adam and Eve lost the protective covering that was over them and could no longer think as God thinks. That is also what happened to John the builder when he built his *home* his way. His reasoning abilities were impeded, and he was eventually destroyed by his pride and refusal to follow sound advice and instructions from his parents and others who loved him deeply.

Be incredibly careful that what you know, believe, and practice is the truth; otherwise, you might be dancing with the devil. Remember, "There is a way that seems right to a man, but its end is the way of death" (*Proverbs 14:12*).

This is the loving message that Jesus presents to all of us. He is still in the carpentry business, only now He is rebuilding lives. Yes, there is a tearing down of the old, which can hurt, but, from that, He can erect a new heart's *home* where the Father, the Son, and the Holy Spirit will come to live. That is His promise, and He cannot lie, and He

114

cannot fail. That is why it is called the Good News. *John 15:4-16* states, in essence, that we are to abide (live) in Him by abiding in His word and love. If we do, He and the Father will make their home in us, and we will be blessed. The verses further state that He is the Good Shepherd who gave His life for the sheep. In our natural state, we are not the sheep of His pasture. His sheep hear His voice and follow Him. They eat healthy food in His pastures of love and holiness. Our diet is what makes us feel good and happy.

We want to be the rulers of our own destiny like our first parents. We are prone to eat harmful food from tainted pastures of "pleasure." That is how deep pride is ingrained in the human soul. It is His passion, however, to set us free from that dark power of evil that lies within every soul born of a woman on Earth. When Jesus died and descended into Hell, He did not suffer there. He took the keys to hell from the defeated Dragon (i.e., Satan) unopposed. Jesus is the key to Life. It is He who, through His Spirit, can unlock that which has bound or imprisoned us.

His desire and passion are to see us in His Heavenly Home one day. He died for us for that very purpose. He rose from the grave in victory to prove that He is the God of love who personally loves all mankind. He is not our enemy. He is the Prince of Peace who is calling out to all of us and saying, "Come to me." "In my Father's house are many mansions, I go to prepare a place for you" (*John 14:12*).

Isaiah 9:6 **is a prophecy about the Christ (Anointed One) coming to Earth. It validates who He is, and it was written about 740 years before Jesus' birth. It is one of scores and scores of verified prophecies about Jesus' birth, life, death, and resurrection written centuries before He was born on Earth as the Son of man. Listen to this mind-blowing word from the book of Isaiah: "For unto us a Child is born, unto us a Son is given; and the government will be upon His shoulder. AND His name will be called Wonderful, Counselor, Mighty God, Everlasting Father, Prince of Peace." The Child/Son is also the Mighty God and the Everlasting Father. WOW!**

Isaiah 7:14 **states, "Therefore, the Lord Himself will give you a sign: behold the virgin shall conceive and bear a Son and shall call His name Immanuel." Immanuel, as noted earlier, means "GOD WITH US."**

Remember that litmus test that I asked you to take? The fact of the matter is that all of us have fallen short of God's glory. He is a Holy God, but we are not a holy people. Because all of us are sinners, just like the builder in this allegory, all of us will pass away one day. *Hebrews 9:27* confirms this: "And as it is appointed for men to die once, but after this the judgment." So, while living on Earth's shores, we should be preparing for our future and permanent *home.* We are not to be flippant or fearful or unbelieving because the God of the universe is on our side, and it is His will that none of us perish (*2 Peter 3:9*). Yet, we still have that awesome free will that He put in us, the ability to choose, to say "yes" or "no."

Have any of you folks been wondering what it (i.e., life) is all about lately? Perhaps there is something that has been stirring inside you. It could be an emptiness that is nagging you. Perhaps you can't seem to pinpoint it. Then, more than likely, it is God at work deep within your heart's home. Those nudges are exactly what the Holy Spirit does. Our friend in this story disregarded every attempt to take that look in that mirror and had to be dealt with in a harsh and radical way to get his attention. Wherever you are, God already knows it.

The author of this allegory at times identified with John Carter more than he would care to admit. You are not alone, dear friend. Satan would like you to think that you are, or that you're okay when you are not. Disregard those thoughts, for they are lies. Remember, that deep inner peace and outward joy are your barometers.

With a smile on His face, He is extending His hand of grace, mercy, forgiveness, and love to you right now. He wants to dance with you. Please respond to His generous offer. It will bring about that significant change that everyone needs.

Chapter Twenty-Three: God and His Passion

This is what the verses quoted in this story are saying to every reader. They are the foundation behind John the builder's life and encounters with death. They are the building blocks of, not only salvation, but also of leading a successful Christian life that shows God's love to our neighbors. As far as the Father is concerned, friends, *everyone* is our neighbor. The Bible declares that Jesus ministered salvation to us while we were yet His enemies and alienated from our Creator. He tells us to have that same kind of love for all the peoples of Earth. By our own power, none of us can do that. That is why Jesus sent us the gift of the Holy Spirit. *Zechariah 4:6* states, "Not by might nor by power, but by my Spirit, says the Lord Almighty."

Only the Holy Spirit can make alive the words of truth in the Bible. It is He who is willing and able to take the words presented here and apply them to our hearts. He is your

Friend. I trust that you will let Him use this booklet to speak to your innermost being (your heart's home) and to let Him accomplish His purposes in your life. I understand that reading *A Close Encounter with the Prince of Darkness* is NOT the same as reading the Bible, but I hope that, by reading it, people will be drawn to the Scriptures that reveal the Father, Son, and Holy Spirit.

I will finish the presentation with two important descriptive writings that reveal both the "what" and the "why" behind Jesus' ministry.

- **"Behold our God"** is a visible description of **what** the Son of God did for us. In this text, the Lord leaves us with free will and choice.

- **"The Passion of the Christ"** is a humble description of **why** He endured what He endured for us. In this text, prayerfully, the Lord Jesus Christ leaves us soft in our hearts and responsive to Him.

Behold our God!

Jesus was

MARRED by man's sin.

SMITTEN by God's hand.

DELIVERED UP for all.

Behold—the Sacrifice of Love!

The Lord was

BRUISED for our hurts.

WOUNDED that we may be healed.

KILLED that we might live.

Behold—the Son of God!

He was

SINLESS, shameless, victorious.

TRUTH was our substitute.

HOLINESS personified.

Behold—our God!

His offer

GRACE is calling now.

FAITH to believe is here.

REPENTANCE: what will it be?

Behold—His mercy!

He weeps

STRANGER, what does this mean to you?

FRIEND, your hour draws near.

SINNER, you have no plea.

Behold—your Judge!

The Passion of the Christ

His HEAD was wounded that our minds would be renewed and think as He does.

His HEART was bruised that ours would be whole and wholly His.

His HANDS were pierced that we would be inscribed on the Father's palms, "Belonging to the Lord."

His HEELS dug into the cross that we would be lifted up and be able to breathe fresh air.

His HONOR was laid low that we would be honorable people.

His HEALTH failed unto death that we would be alive and healthy.

His HAPPINESS was complete at death because He saw us hidden within Himself, a gift unto God the Father.

His HEAVEN became a reality when He rose from the grave in victory over sin and recreated us in His image.

His HOLINESS is now ours. His love flowing out to others.

CLOSING COMMENTS

This book will have had no effect if the reader simply views it from the outside in. Its only value is if it has read us from the inside out and the response of our souls to the veracity of the words is "Yes, Lord, yes!" So many of the verses quoted here could have been exchanged for others. The Bible repeats its theme and purpose over and over in both the Old Testament and the New Testament. That theme is, "'I love you,' says the Lord, 'but we have a problem here'."

John, the main character in this discourse, had parents and others in his life who accepted the Word of God and faithfully tried to live it. They were not perfect people, but they were part of His family and tried to show him the way. By living his life his way, John was, in fact, proving God's Word to be true. His rejection of Jesus who is the Way, the Truth, and the Life and the only way to the Father (*John 14*:6) left him an easy target for the one who wanted to devour his soul.

John Carter's plight was the same as that of all those who have heard Jesus' words but rejected them and, hence, rejected Jesus. Listen to this, dear reader. In *John 10:25-30*, Jesus tells unbelievers that the works (i.e., teachings with miracles) that He did were done in His Father's name. Those works bore witness to Him. The reason that they did not believe was because they were not of His flock. He was offering that crowd of people eternal life through Him, and they said no, even after He told them that no one would be able to snatch them out of His Father's hand. He closes that claim by making a statement that no other religious leader could make. He says, **"I and the Father are one"** (*John 10:30*). They rejected Him as many others down through the ages have—but what about you, folks? Where is your *heart's home* today?

So, is this endeavor on my part simply an allegory about a fictional person and his being a hardheaded as well as a hardhearted fool, or is it about God's Word versus *our* desire to be the master of *our* own destiny? Some of you may be nicer people than others but still have that significant need that was discussed throughout John Carter's encounter.

We must get off the throne of our lives, folks, and let Him sit there if we want to get right with Him and live a successful life in Christ Jesus. How do we do that if we do not recognize that our *home* was marred and defiled from the get-go? Christianity is not an opiate, as has been claimed. The opiates that soothe our guilty conscience are thoughts such as "I am not that bad of a person; I work hard and don't bother others; I help people and give money to the church—I, I, I." The "**I**" **factor** has become the central focus. In other words, if this factor had any significance, gaining heaven would be based on how good we think we are and how we feel rather than on what Jesus did for us when He suffered and died in our place.

I mentioned what happened to our first parents. Read the story of the encounter they had with the Prince of Darkness. It can be found in *Genesis 3*. Adam and Eve 'danced with the devil' and lost. Again, please let me reiterate this fact. Their fallen nature has been passed down to ALL of us. It is part of our DNA. There are no exceptions. No human ever born can close the gap between God and his or her tainted state by following the rigid rules that come with a works-based "religion." How can imperfect humans form any religion that would please a perfect God? How can people follow the dictates of any religious leader who himself is just another sinful human? Paul, who wrote most of the epistles in the New Testament said, "Imitate [i.e., follow me] **AS** I follow Christ." (*1 Corinthians 11:1*). It is through Christ and Christ alone that we become reunited with the Father.

In *Psalm 51:1-17*, King David confesses in detail a horrible sin that he committed. It was a capital crime that called for his death. God heard his genuinely penitential plea and granted him His grace, mercy, forgiveness, and restoration. God's definition of Love is different from ours. Ours is often based on how people treat us. His definition is to love those that are not worthy of His adoration—those who are, in fact, His enemies. Remember, folks, that Christ Jesus died for us while we were yet sinners. That should tell us two things: one, we are sinners, and two, it was Christ who saved us and not we ourselves.

The same grace of God that is explained in the Scriptures and this story is being offered to you right now. *A Close Encounter with the Prince of Darkness* is a fictional tale, but the Prince of Darkness is not fictional, nor is our tainted human nature. Please take advantage of God's offer and come to, or return to, the Alpha and the Omega, the "Beginning and the End," the One who is and who was and who is to come, the Almighty (*Revelation 1:8*). He is a miracle-working God, and no one is beyond His reach, if they in faith reach out to Him.

If you folks would read carefully the love story presented in the Prodigal Son account found in *Luke 15: 11-32*, you would not only see John Carter's story but perhaps see a lost daughter or son that are out in the wilderness of their own making. Never, no, never give up on them. Not even on your death bed. Especially note the attitude of the Prodigal sons brother, who in his own way, had a hard heart of bitterness, hatred, unforgiveness, self-righteousness. He was in worse shape than his broken brother, spiritually speaking because he set himself up as a judge and did not think he needed a significant change.

In closing, I ask you to meditate on **"the Passion of the Christ."** Even though, as mere mortals, we cannot fully grasp the depth of His suffering, how can we deny or lay aside such pure love being poured out for all fallen humanity? On the cross, holiness was exchanged for unholiness. Death was exchanged for life. Defeat was exchanged for victory. He is risen and promises His faithful children that they too will rise again.

Oh, by the way, if you are a Christian, one other important thing needs to be mentioned. You need to include being exceedingly thankful and grateful for all that He has done. This will bring forth genuine praise, which, in turn, will cause you to be joyful, happy, and relaxed. All His people are to delight themselves in Him and to rest in Him. If you read *Psalm 37:1-8*, you will see among those powerful admonitions and instructions verses that state that we are to delight in the Lord as well as to rest in Him. That is what His love and peace bring to those who are heading to **HIS HOME.**

We may not think that being joyful and happy will translate into humor, but it absolutely will. It will prevent us from becoming stuffed-shirt Christians. It is part of God's character and nature. He put the ability for us to have joy and a humorous side within us when we were created. That means that He, too, laughs at something that is funny—if it is wholesome and clean.

Yes, it may be somewhat stormy out there from time to time, and you may be going through a lot of "stuff" at this time in your life, but a joyful Christian will uplift and bless others. "The joy of the Lord is our strength" (*Nehemiah* 8:10).

HIS GRACE, HIS MERCY, HIS LOVE,

HIS PLAN, HIS POWER.

***HIS SACRIFICE.* HE DID IT ALL.**

WHERE THEN IS OUR BOASTING?

EPHESIANS 2:8-9. TITUS 3:5-7.

Biography

Jerry has been married to his wife Jane for sixty-two years. They have five children, ten grandchildren, and three great-grandchildren. He was a police officer in the NYPD for twenty-five years. His entire career was spent as a patrol officer serving the people of that city

It was in his thirteenth year that he had a dramatic conversion to Christ. While there have been some rough spots over the years, he has never doubted that he is loved by his Heavenly Father. He knows that he is a work-in-progress and thanks the Lord for His grace, mercy, and patience.

His passion is to see people from all backgrounds, beliefs, and conditions take an honest look in the mirror of their lives and ask themselves whether they are in the right relationship with their Creator or are building their eternal home *their way*.

This booklet is dedicated to the Lord for the very purpose of exposing the truth about Him so that people will have an opportunity to either give their hearts to Jesus or to return to that first Love they had when they first got saved.

"Christ in me the hope of glory." (*Colossians 1:27*).

If this book spoke to your heart, please leave a review on Amazon,

https://www.amazon.com/Close-Encounter-Prince-Darkness-ebook/dp/B0B8G5TXPR/

To get in touch with the author:

GeraldFrancis1013@gmail.com

Made in the USA
Columbia, SC
20 March 2023